To: Justin

from: Michelle &
       Lara

D1071616

2015

The Goblin's Toyshop
and
Other Stories

by
ENID BLYTON

Illustrated by
Lesley Smith

AWARD PUBLICATIONS

For further information on Enid Blyton please visit *www.blyton.com*

ISBN 978-1-84135-470-5

First published by Sampson Low (now part of Simon & Schuster
Young Books) as *Enid Blyton's Holiday Book Series*

First published by Award Publications Limited 1994
This edition first published 2006

Published by Award Publications Limited,
The Old Riding School, The Welbeck Estate,
Worksop, Nottinghamshire, S80 3LR

12 5

Printed in the United Kingdom

CONTENTS

The Goblin's Toyshop

"There's a new toyshop at the end of the village!" cried the pixie children one day. "Come and see!" So they all went, and pressed their turned-up noses against the toyshop window. "Oooh," they said, in delight. "What beautiful dolls! And look at that smart wooden soldier – and oh, that bear with twinkling eyes!"

"There aren't any trains," said little Pop-off, mournfully. He did so like trains.

"And no bricks," said Jinks, who liked building little houses.

"But see the sailor dolls and the baby dolls and the dressed-up toy cats and dogs!" said Fenny. "Oh, I wish my money-box was full."

The goblin who had just opened the new toyshop came to the door. He had bright green eyes and such pointed ears that they looked as sharp as arrows. He gave the children a grin that stretched from ear to ear.

"Well, children, I hope I shall see you on your birthdays and at Christmastime, and every Saturday, too. You'll find my toys are far cheaper to buy than anyone else's!"

He was quite right. The pixie children could get a toy soldier for a pound, and a big teddy bear with a growl in his middle for one pound fifty. The dolls were all the same price, five pounds each. It was marvellous.

It was no wonder that all the children of Cherry Village spent their money at the goblin toyshop. They bought dolls and soldiers and bears and dogs and cats. But they couldn't buy trains or bricks or ships or tops because the goblin didn't sell them.

"I'm not interested in those," he said, with his wide grin. "I only sell the toys I really like."

And then, after he had sold a few dozen dolls and soldiers and bears, something peculiar happened. First

Jinks' toy soldiers disappeared. Then
Fenny's two new dolls went. Then Pop-
off's blue teddy bear vanished. Binkie's
toy dog wasn't on the windowsill one
morning, where he had left it the night
before, and Gobbo's sailor doll had gone
from the toy cupboard. How strange!

Nobody could find out what had
happened. They hunted all over the

place, but the toys were not found again. "Some thief must have passed through our village in the night, and stolen all the children's new toys," said the pixies mournfully.

Next night somebody's ragdoll disappeared, and three dolls. And then a toy dog vanished and a baby doll too. How very peculiar!

The pixies went to the goblin about it. "Can you tell us what is happening?" they said, puzzled. "Our children's toys are all going one by one."

"Strange," said the goblin, shaking his head. "Very, very strange. I have no idea where the toys have gone – but as the children are so sad about it, please come to my shop with them and they shall have any toy they please at half price!"

"How kind you are!" said the pixies, pleased, and they bought a great many new toys from the green-eyed goblin. But before long those toys disappeared at night, too, and nobody knew what was happening.

Then one night, little Fenny, who had three new dolls, decided that one of them had a bad cold and must be undressed and go to bed. So she undressed her, took off all her clothes and her shoes and stockings, put a little nightie on her, and popped her into bed.

That night two of her dolls disappeared – but not the one she had put to bed with a cold!

Her brother heard Fenny crying and came to see what the matter was. He looked puzzled when he heard that one of the dolls hadn't disappeared. Now why should the thief steal two, but leave the one in the cot?

"Fenny," he whispered, "I am going to watch for the thief! I shall hide in the wood and watch the lane that runs through the village. Whoever creeps down there at night will be the thief! I am sure he will have an armful of toys!"

"No – don't watch, Tippy," said Fenny, frightened. "You know everyone thinks it's a very powerful wizard, who comes at night and makes himself invisible so that no one sees him. And that's how he takes our toys – putting his invisible hand into our windows."

"There's something strange about this," said Tippy. "I'm going to watch!"

So that night he hid in the wood and kept an eye on the lane that ran through the sleeping village. Nobody came. And then, just as Tippy was going to creep home, he heard a tiny sound. Tippitty-tap, tippitty-tap – and down the lane came a very tiny figure indeed. What could it be? A dwarf wizard? A pygmy magician?

Then he stared in astonishment. It was no wizard – but just a toy soldier, walking quickly down the lane in his little clicking shoes – tippitty-tap!

And then came a doll, and after that a soft-walking toy cat, dressed in skirt and shawl. She had shoes on her feet but she made no sound. Then came a curly-haired doll and two more toy soldiers! Tippy could hardly believe his eyes.

He called out in a whisper: "Hey, Soldier! Hey, Sailor Doll! What are you doing?"

But they took no notice at all. Not one of them even looked round, but went quietly on their way. They were toys that could walk, but they didn't seem to be alive.

Tippy got up quietly and followed a fat teddy bear down the lane. The bear walked steadily on, his shoes making a little shuffling noise because he didn't lift up his feet properly. And, to Tippy's great surprise, he walked in at the open

gate of the goblin toyshop, went up the little path, and in at the door. It must be open then!

Tippy crept up to the door, too. It was ajar. Inside a tiny light was burning. One by one the toys went to a little shelf and sat themselves down. They were quite still then and didn't move at all.

Tippy looked round cautiously. He could hear someone snoring in the next room. That must be the goblin. He caught sight of a box with something printed on the lid. Tippy bent over it, trying to make out what was written there.

"Walking spells for shoes," he read in astonishment, and then he suddenly guessed the secret of the disappearing toys!

That wicked goblin! He sold toys that wore shoes – he didn't sell trains or bricks or ships because they didn't wear shoes and couldn't walk. But soldiers and teddies and dolls could all wear shoes!

"So he pops a walking spell into their shoes, knowing that at a certain time the spell will work – and all the toys will walk back to him, so that he can sell them once again!" thought Tippy. "Oh, he's bad. He's a fraud! But how clever he is!"

Tippy sat and wondered what to do. Then he caught sight of the goblin's boots standing by the door, and he suddenly grinned. He opened the box and took out a handful of the walking spells. He pressed them right into the

15

toes of the boots. Then he crept out.

Next day everyone in the village knew about the goblin's mean trick. They crowded to his shop angrily, and he met them with his usual grin.

"What nonsense!" he said, when they had shouted to tell him what they knew. "I know nothing about walking-spells, nothing at all. I have never even heard of them. There are no such things. Tippy dreamt it all."

"Pack up your things, you wicked goblin, and go!" shouted the pixies.

"Certainly not," said the green-eyed fellow. "I shall stay here as long as I like. Nothing can make me leave – and I warn you – be careful in case I put a bad spell on you all."

16

But, as he spoke, his feet began to twist about and wriggle to and fro. The goblin gazed down at them in surprise. What was happening?

Tippy gave a chuckle. *He* knew. The handful of walking-spells was beginning to work! And very soon the goblin found his feet walking him out of his cottage and down the path to his front gate. "Stop feet, stop!" he yelled. "What's the matter with you?"

"The same thing that was the matter with the feet of all the toys you sold!" cried Tippy, in delight. "Walking-spells in your boots – but I forgot – you've never heard of such things, have you!"

The pixies ran beside the furious, bewildered goblin till he came to the end of the village. Then they said:

"Goodbye! You've so many spells in your boots that you won't stop walking till you get to the Land of Goodness Knows Where! We shan't see *you* again, Goblin!"

They didn't, of course, because he had to walk for years. What a wonderful time the children had in the toyshop!

"The toys are yours," said Mr Plod, the policeman. "The goblin cheated you of many dolls and other toys. Now take what you want. He will never, never come back."

So the children took all the toys they wanted – but what was the first thing they did to them? Can you guess? Yes – they took off all the toys' shoes! They weren't going to have them walking away again!

The Little
Chatterbox

There was once a little girl who never stopped talking. That sounds funny, but I expect you know people like that, don't you? We are always saying to them: "Dear me, *what* a chatterbox you are! Do stop talking for a minute!"

Well, Paula was like that. Nobody could stop her talking. She began when she woke up in the morning, she went on all the day, and she was still talking when her mother put her to bed at night.

This is how she talked, without stopping: "You know, I really must tell you, yesterday I saw a dog with such a long tail, and when it wagged it made quite a wind, and I patted it, but it ran away, so I went on to school, and when I got there I was just in time, of course I've never been late, well, I changed my shoes and I took my pencil-box and went into school, and that morning I got all my sums right, and the teacher said my writing was very good, and I got top marks in drawing, and the teacher said I was very good at animals, and I daresay when I grow up I shall be an artist and make a lot of money, and if I do I shall buy Mummy a beautiful car and Daddy a splendid pipe, and Baby the best rattle in the world, and Auntie Susan a new dress, and ..."

That was how Paula talked, on and on and on without stopping. "Oh, Paula, *stop*!" people would say. "You really are a terrible chatterbox."

Well, it is very nice to be able to talk easily, but no one likes to hear another person talking all the time. "It's selfish, Paula," said Peter, who wanted to tell her about his new book. "Stop a minute. I've got something to say too!"

"Wait till I've finished," Paula would say – and, of course, she never would finish, and Peter would go off with his book to find someone else to show it to.

Sometimes Mummy had a headache. "Paula, stop chattering," she would say. "My head aches and you make it worse. Be quiet for a little while, dear."

But Paula wouldn't. Her tongue wagged on and on and on, and at last her mother would go out of the room and leave her talking to herself.

But she often woke up the baby with her endless talking. He would cry loudly and Mummy would come running out. "Oh, Paula dear – surely

you haven't been talking loudly and waking Baby up! There's no one here to talk to!"

"I was talking to my dolls," said Paula. If she had no boy or girl or grown-up to talk to, she would talk to her toys. Really there was no stopping that tongue of hers!

One day she went for a walk on Pixie Hill. Some of the children said they had seen pixies there, dressed in yellow and green, like tiny men, but Paula never had, and she didn't believe it.

All the same, there were some there

that day, and two of them met Paula as she walked up the hill. They said good morning to her, and Paula began her usual chatter.

How she chattered!

The little men tried to say something every now and again, but it wasn't a bit of good. Paula didn't even *try* to listen, she loved the sound of her own voice so much.

"What funny little men you are!" she began, with a laugh. "Why do you wear hats like that? I once had a hat like yours when I went to a fancy-dress party, and it had a red feather in it, and everyone said it was the best hat there, and I won the prize for the best fancy dress, and the prize was a beautiful

paint-box, and you really should have seen the pictures I painted with those paints, they were beautiful, and –"

"Wait a minute," began one little man, trying to get a few words in quickly.

But Paula went on without stopping.

"And when I took my pictures to school the next day the teacher was very pleased, and she pinned them all up on the wall and –"

"I want to say something," said the second pixie, but still Paula swept on and on.

"And all the children thought they were wonderful, so when I'm grown up I expect I shall be an artist and make a lot of money, and –"

The two little men suddenly pounced on Paula. One of them tied his big handkerchief round the little girl's mouth. Paula was surprised and angry, and her voice came gurgling out through the handkerchief.

"Ooogle, obble, oogle, obble, oogle, oogle!"

24

"Now listen!" said the first little man to Paula. "We want to know something. We've been sent out of pixie-town to buy a musical box for the little Prince Dreamy, who is ill. We know that a musical box is a sort of box in which music and voices are kept, and you can turn them on when you want to hear them. Are you a musical box?"

"Ooogle, obble, oogle, obble," answered poor Paula. A small pixie ran up to see what was the matter. He laughed when he saw Paula.

"Ho," he said. "You've caught a chatterbox, have you? Well, she'll go on talking for days and days if you let her.

She's the finest chatterbox in the world!"

"A chatterbox!" said one little man to another. "Oooh! Perhaps a chatterbox is as good as a musical box. Will she really talk without stopping? We want something like that to keep little Prince Dreamy amused."

"Well, take Paula then," said the small pixie. "Put her into a box with a nice lid, and she'll do very well for a musical box. You won't have to wind her up as you would have to do with a musical box, and she'll never, never run down!"

"My goodness, what a fine idea!" said

26

the two little men. They took the hanky away from Paula's mouth, and tied her hands behind her back instead. She began talking hard at once.

"You let me go, you naughty little creatures, or I'll tell Mummy, and she will tell the policeman and he will come and take you to prison, and then you will be locked up and you will be very sorry you caught a nice little girl like me, who hasn't done you any harm, and who doesn't want to go with you and see Prince Dreamy, whoever he is, he doesn't sound very exciting, anyway, and ..."

All the time she was talking the little men trotted her down the hill to a little blue door set far into a cave in the

hillside. In they went and down some steps lighted by big candles swinging from the roof. Down and down, and then up and up – and at last into a big palace full of fairy and pixie servants, who were all very surprised to see Paula.

"Where's the palace carpenter?" asked one of the little men. "We want him."

"He's in the workroom," said an elf. The little men hurried Paula off to a big workroom, where a tall gnome was standing, working at a new rocking-horse for the little prince.

"We've found a real live chatterbox," said the men excitedly. "She'll do awfully well for a musical box. Make her a box with a lid quickly, carpenter, and we'll put her in and take her to the little prince."

In no time at all the carpenter made a beautiful green box, rather like a tall cupboard, with a hinged lid on top. Paula was lifted in, and she was carried quickly away to the bedroom of the

little sick prince. The lid was shut, so Paula could not see or hear anything. She was very angry, and she talked loudly at the top of her voice, but no one could hear her with the lid shut.

The queen was in the room, and a nurse. The little prince lay on his bed. He was not allowed to sit up. He was

not allowed to read. So he had asked for a musical box that he could turn on and off and listen to whenever he wished.

"Your Majesty," said one of the pixies in an excited voice, "we have had such a piece of luck. We couldn't get a musical box anywhere, however hard we tried – but we managed to get a real live chatterbox! Here it is. Inside this box is a voice that goes on and on and on without stopping, telling all sorts of things. If you want to hear it, lift the lid; if you don't, shut it down!"

30

"How splendid!" said the queen. She lifted the lid and out came Paula's voice at once.

"And if you think I'm going to stay in this box all day long you're wrong, because I won't, I shall escape, and I shall run home, and fetch my daddy and my mummy, and they'll come here to this palace and scold you all, and I can tell you, when Mummy scolds

31

anyone it's dreadful. Why, I remember once she scolded my little cousin so hard for breaking two windows that he cried all down his overall and made it so wet that he had to take it off and dry it. Of course, I never cry like that, I'm not so silly, and, anyway, my eyes get red and swollen and I look ugly, and nobody likes looking ugly, especially when they're quite pretty like me, I've often been told I'm pretty, in fact, I'm a nice little girl and why I should be in this box I don't know; it's a naughty thing to put me here and ..."

The little prince lay and listened in

delight. The voice went on and on, telling all kinds of things, silly little things, amusing little things, things that were strange and surprising to a fairy prince who had lived all his life in a palace.

"This musical box is lovely," he said to his mother. "Let me keep it. It's a most wonderful chatterbox, really it is. I could listen all day long!"

The queen and the nurse were pleased to see Prince Dreamy so happy. They went out of the room and left him to listen to the endless voice coming out of the box.

Magic kept Paula inside that box. It was impossible to get out. All she could do was to talk, and talk she did. She talked all day long, and grew very angry when she heard Prince Dreamy having

33

his dinner and his tea, for no one gave her anything to eat or drink at all. They didn't think that musical boxes needed food.

When night came the queen shut down the lid, so that the voice was no longer heard, and the prince could go to sleep. Early in the morning he awoke and opened the lid again, and at once the voice came out, rather weak and small and tired, but still chattering away.

"If only you'll let me out, I'll never, never chatter so much again, only let me out and you'll see I will really stop, and listen to other people."

"Oh, I shan't let you out then!" cried the little prince. "I don't want you to stop! I'm going to keep you here for always, my own real, live chatterbox!"

What a shock that was for poor little chatterbox Paula. She was so frightened at the idea of staying in the chatterbox for always that she lost her voice. She couldn't speak a word. She stayed quite silent – and even when she found her voice again she didn't say a word. Perhaps if she was quiet the prince wouldn't want her and she could go!

She didn't say a word all day, and that was very hard for her. The prince soon got tired of a silent musical box, or Chatter-Box as he called it, and told his nurse to take it away. She carried it out of the room, slipped over a rug and fell down. The box fell too, the lid shot open and out slid Paula.

In a second she was on her feet, running for all she was worth. Down the steps into the hillside she went, along the dark passage, up more steps and out on the sunny, windy hillside. She fled home, sobbing, hungry and thirsty.

"Where *have* you been, darling?" cried her mother. "We've been hunting for you all night. Where *have* you been?"

"I've been a musical box. I was put inside a big Chatter-Box!" wept Paula. "It was all because I talked so much. I never will again, Mummy, never!"

And she doesn't. She listens to other people now, and she doesn't go on and on all day long. It was really such a shock to her to be a real, live chatter-box. I should hate it too, wouldn't you?

The
Peculiar Boots

There was once an impatient pixie who expected everyone to be as quick as himself. His name was Lightfoot, and it suited him well, for he was very quick and light on his feet.

"Lightfoot never walks, he always runs!" said his friends, with a laugh. "Look – there he goes, rushing along as usual!"

And there, sure enough, was Lightfoot, hurrying down the village street to do his shopping. But how he hated having to walk slowly behind prams, or behind the old women who went to market each day! How he hated having to walk along with old Father Tap Tap, who had to go slowly because of his poor bad leg!

Lightfoot lived with his aunt Snow-White. She had snow-white hair, and was gentle and kind. She used to get cross with Lightfoot because he was so impatient with those who were slower than himself.

"Lightfoot, old people can't help being slow," she would say. "They cannot hurry as you can. Wait till you are old, Lightfoot, and you will soon see how hard it is to hurry or to rush."

"Oh, when I'm old I shall be just as quick as I am now," said Lightfoot scornfully. "You won't see me hobbling along, holding everybody up on the pavement because I am so slow! Indeed you won't!"

He went out and slammed the door, a thing that his aunt Snow-White hated. He ran down the street in a hurry, nearly knocking over Mrs Jinky and her pram.

"Bother prams!" said Lightfoot. "Bother all slow people! I don't like them a bit. I believe they are slow on purpose!"

The pavement was crowded with people doing their shopping. Just in front of Lightfoot was an old dame he didn't know. She plodded along slowly, helping herself with a stick. She was big and tall, and Lightfoot tried to push past her. She turned and looked at him angrily.

"Now, now! Who is this, so impatient behind me? What! A young pixie like you pushing an old woman to make her go more quickly! How dare you!"

"Well, you are so slow!" said Lightfoot rudely. "I'm in a hurry. I believe old people are slow just so that they can stop people like me going along quickly."

"What you want is a good lesson," began the old dame, rapping her stick on the pavement. But Lightfoot wasn't going to listen to any lecture. No – he pushed by her and ran down the street as fast as he could go!

He did his shopping and then he thought he would go for a walk on the nearby common, which was a blaze of

golden gorse. Off he went, and had a lovely time smelling the delicious gorse-scent, and singing to the rabbits that popped out of their holes. Then he felt tired, so he lay down by a gorse-bush and fell fast asleep. He didn't see the old woman come slowly by. He didn't hear her say, "Oho! Here is that horrid pixie!"

He didn't feel her slip off his pixie-shoes and put them into her bag. He didn't see her put down a pair of fine-looking red boots beside him. No, he was fast asleep.

But when he awoke, how surprised he was to find his shoes gone and the beautiful boots standing in their place! He sat up in delight.

"Ah! A present from somebody! How lovely!" said Lightfoot, and he put on the boots at once. They fitted so tightly that he was quite surprised. He stood

42

up and walked a few steps. Yes – there was no doubt about it at all, the boots looked simply grand!

He began to walk home, hoping that everyone would admire his boots. But there was suddenly something very peculiar about them. They felt dreadfully heavy – so heavy that Lightfoot could hardly walk along.

"Goodness! They feel as if they are made of iron or something!" said Lightfoot in amazement. "I can't bear it. I shall take them off!"

But he couldn't take them off! They fitted so very, very tightly that it was quite impossible to tug them off his feet. They simply wouldn't come! So he had to go on walking in them.

They hurt him because they were so tight. They hurt his toes, they hurt his heels, they hurt his ankles. They felt as heavy as lead! It was dreadful! Lightfoot found that he could only just hobble along, very, very slowly indeed.

"If only I had a stick!" he groaned. "That would help me!" So he cut

himself a stick from the hedge and helped himself along with that. Hobble, hobble, hobble, he went, just like an old, old man.

Everyone stared at him. Why, here was Lightfoot, who always ran and never walked, hobbling slowly along with a stick! Whatever had happened to him?

Everyone was kind to him. They came and asked him what was the matter. They gave him an arm across the road. They helped him up the hill. They were as kind as they could be, and were not a bit impatient with him.

44

Only one person was not kind. That was the old woman who had exchanged Lightfoot's shoes for the boots. She was there in the town and she smiled to herself as she saw Lightfoot hobbling past.

"You must have suddenly become old," she said to him as he passed. "Is it nice to have heavy, slow feet, Lightfoot? Is it nice to be slow when you want to be quick?"

Lightfoot went red. He remembered that he had been rude to the old woman. He had pushed her. Now he was walking even more slowly than she

45

had been. He said nothing, but hobbled home to his aunt Snow-White. She listened very gravely when he told her everything.

"I'm afraid those are magic boots," she said, looking at them. "They have been given to you to teach you a lesson, Lightfoot. They will fall off when you have learnt the lesson!"

So for a whole week poor Lightfoot had to hobble painfully about in the heavy, tight boots, and his feet hurt him so much that he could hardly get along. But his friends were very kind and patient with him and helped him all they could.

And at the end of the week, Lightfoot had learnt his lesson! "I am very sorry I ever was rude or impatient with old or slow people," he said. "I know what it is like now to have slow feet that won't hurry, however much I want them to. And my friends have been so kind to me – far kinder than I ever was to old people myself! I am really ashamed of myself."

And as soon as he said that, the boots fell off his feet, broke into bits and disappeared! Oh, how glad Lightfoot was to see them go! Now he could run and jump again, now he could hurry!

He hurries as much as ever – but he is sweet with old people now, and helps them along all he can. "I'm lucky to be young and quick," he says to them. "Let me help you!" It's no wonder they all love to see Lightfoot hurrying along down the street to meet them!

The
Wonderful Doll

"Sarah! Louise! Pam! You simply *must* come and see my wonderful doll after tea today," said Alice.

"What's so wonderful about her?" asked Pam.

"She can talk *and* walk – all by herself!" said Alice. "Perhaps you don't believe me – but I tell you she can."

"Is she alive, then?" asked Sarah, astonished.

"Oh, no. She's just a doll. But if I wind her up she'll talk and walk. Do come after tea and see," said Alice.

So after tea Sarah, Louise and Pam went round to Alice's house to see the wonderful doll. She really was as marvellous as Alice had said.

Alice wound her up at the back and

somehow that set off a little talking machine in the doll's body, and the doll suddenly began to cry out, like a baby.

"Mummy! Mummy! I want you. Pick me up, Mummy. I want you!"

The three visitors were really startled. They stared at the doll as if they couldn't believe their eyes.

"Good gracious!" said Pam. "She's got a real, proper voice. Now make her walk."

Alice stood her up. The doll balanced herself perfectly, and then put out one foot. She began to walk, rather stiffly – but certainly walked! She walked all the way round the table and back, and then called out again:

"Mummy! Mummy! I want you. Pick me up, Mummy. I want you!"

Alice picked her up and loved her. Her eyes shone. "There you are, you see! You didn't believe me – but I spoke the truth, didn't I? She *does* walk and talk!"

All the toys were amazed at the new doll. It was all very well to come alive and talk toy-language at night – but to be able to walk and talk when you hadn't even come alive to play at night was very strange.

"She must be alive," said the clown, talking to the teddy-bear at night. "She can't be a proper doll like the others are. They *have* to sit still and be silent all day – but not this doll. She talks just like a real child."

They were rather afraid of the new doll. She talked to them at night in a proper toy-voice, but they still felt very awkward with her. They didn't make friends, and the new doll was rather sad.

"You're so peculiar," said the teddy-bear. "We can't seem to get used to you, new doll. You don't seem quite to belong to us, somehow."

"But I *do* belong," said the new doll. "I can't help being able to walk and talk. It's only clockwork. I'm a toy just as you are. Do be friends."

"Well – I expect we'll be friends when we've got used to you," said the clown.

51

"I don't want to wait till you've got used to me," said the new doll sadly. "But I suppose I must."

Now, two days after that, something very frightening happened in the playroom. It was in the afternoon and the playroom was empty except for the toys. They sat around, waiting for the night to come, when they could come alive and play. The frightening thing happened all at once. There was a fire in the grate, and three logs were blazing cheerfully. Suddenly there was a loud POP and one of the logs shot a burning piece of wood out of the fire. It landed right in the wastepaper basket.

In a second the paper there had flared up tremendously. The toys watched in horror. Flames! Smoke! Crackle! What were they to do? The curtains would catch fire next.

The new doll sat up. She stood up. She put one foot in front of the other – and she began to walk by herself, just as she usually did.

As she walked she called out in her very-real voice: "Mummy! Mummy! I want you. Pick me up, Mummy. I want you!"

She walked to the door. It was open and she walked out of it into the passage beyond. She came to the top of the stairs. Oh dear – could she possibly walk down those?

She got down one stair and then another, and another. All the time she cried out piteously:

"Mummy! Mummy! I want you. Pick me up, Mummy. I want you!"

The toys heard her calling this out as she went slowly and carefully downstairs. She got to the bottom at last. She walked down the passage and found an open door. She went in, still calling out.

Alice was there, with her mother. They both stared in amazement at the walking, talking doll. Alice leapt up and ran to her. She picked her up.

"What is it, darling? You sound so scared and upset. Has anything up in the playroom frightened you? Mummy, she's come to fetch me, I know she has."

"Don't be silly, dear," said Mummy. "Someone has wound her up and let her walk into the room just to give you a surprise."

"I want you!" cried the doll. "I want you, Mummy! Mummy!"

"Why did you come to fetch me?" asked Alice. "What happened up in the playroom? I'll come and see."

She ran up with the doll in her arms – and as she reached the playroom door a great cloud of smoke billowed out. She screamed.

"Mummy! The playroom's on fire! Quick! Quick!"

Mummy ran up, and as soon as she saw the wastepaper basket burning and the curtains just about to burn she raced into the bathroom. She filled a pail with water and threw it on the burning wastepaper basket.

SIZZLE! SIZZLE! The fire was out. The toys could have cried for joy. Mummy soon cleared up the mess and put a guard round the fire.

"You see, Mummy! My new doll came down on purpose to warn us," said Alice, hugging the doll tightly. "She's wonderful. She walked all the way downstairs, calling out to me. I do love her!"

And after that the toys loved her, too! You should have seen the way they crowded round her that night, patting her on the back and hugging her. What a fuss they made!

So now she's happy because she has plenty of friends. As for Alice, you can guess how she ran to school the next morning, to tell this wonderful tale to Sarah, Louise and Pam! It soon got round to me, of course, and I thought I really *must* tell it to you.

The Enchanted
Button

Once there was a little cheat called
Crooky the Goblin. He was very clever,
so he managed to make a lot of money
by his cheating. He kept a little shop
and sold nearly everything.

He cheated in nasty little ways. He
put in a bad potato or two when Dame
Flip called for a basketful. He sold old
eggs for new when he could. And he put
a few little pebbles into the chicken-
food that Mother Grumps had from
him, for he knew she would never
notice the pebbles when she threw the
grain to her hens – and certainly the
birds wouldn't say anything about
them!

Now one day Witch See-a-Lot felt
certain that Crooky had cheated her

57

over some fruit. Certainly he weighed it out under her eyes, but he must have taken one or two of the plums out of the bag when he twisted it up.

"I'll give him an enchanted button," said Witch See-a-Lot, with a grin. "That'll puzzle him a bit – and if he's a cheat, we shall soon know it!"

So the next time that Dame Flap took Crooky's dirty washing home to do, Witch See-a-Lot watched for it to be put on the line to dry. Dame Flap lived next door, so it was quite easy to see it blowing there.

When Witch See-a-Lot saw Crooky's blue shirt drying in the breeze, and knew that Dame Flap had gone out to do her shopping, she grinned to herself. She took up her button-box, her needle and cotton and her scissors, and out she went into her garden. She climbed over the wall and jumped down into Dame Flap's yard.

Then she went to where Crooky's blue shirt was blowing on the line. She snipped off a button, and then sewed on

one of her own, which really looked exactly like the one she had taken off. As she sewed she chanted a strange little spell:

"Button, dear, if Crooky cheats,
Shout it out to all he meets!
Put him in a dreadful fix,
Make him stop his cheating tricks!"

She snapped off the cotton, and climbed back over the wall, chuckling loudly. Crooky was going to have a fright!

59

Of course, Dame Flap didn't know anything about it at all. She ironed the shirt and took it back to Crooky the same evening. He put it on clean the next day, and did up all the buttons.

Now that morning into the shop came Mother Jinks. She wanted a pound of tea. She didn't look at the scales as Crooky weighed out the tea, so he gave her a little less than a pound. But as he was wrapping it up, a little high voice under his chin yelled out loudly:

"Isn't he a cheat! That isn't a pound

of tea! *I* watched him weigh it out!"

Crooky almost dropped the parcel in fright. He looked all round to see who had spoken. Mother Jinks stared in astonishment. She was puzzled.

"Put that tea on the scales again," she said suddenly. So Crooky had to – and, of course, it didn't weigh a pound.

"So you *did* cheat me!" said Mother Jinks in disgust. "Well, keep your tea! I'll get what I want at the Pixie Stores over the way." And out she walked.

Crooky was puzzled and frightened. Who had shouted out at him? Who could it have been? He hunted all round the shop, and then he heard a little chuckle under his chin:

"I can see you but you can't see me! You're a cheat, that's what you are, Crooky!"

Crooky nearly jumped out of his skin. He felt in his pockets to see if there was anything magic there, but there wasn't.

"I don't like this," he said. "I think I'll just go out delivering potatoes to Father Lucky – and then maybe

whatever spell is in the shop this morning will fly away."

So off he went with his barrow and potatoes. But, of course, he still had on his shirt, and he took that enchanted button with him. It was the top one, just under his chin.

When he got to Father Lucky's, he put a sack of potatoes in the old man's shed. Father Lucky was out, so, as there was no one to see him, Crooky put his hand into the sack and took out a few of the biggest potatoes. He knew

that Father Lucky would never bother to weigh the sack.

The button didn't say a word. "Ha!" thought Crooky, "I expect the magic *was* in the shop, then."

He went back home, and on the way he met Father Lucky. "I've just taken your sack of potatoes," said Crooky to him. "Finest potatoes I've had. You owe me three pounds, please."

"He took out some of the biggest potatoes," shouted the button. "He's a cheat. Don't you believe him, Father Lucky. Don't you pay him till you get home and weigh that sack."

Father Lucky stared at Crooky in the greatest astonishment. He couldn't *imagine* where the voice came from!

63

"I think I *will* weigh that sack before I pay you, Crooky," he said. "And if you *have* cheated me, I'll get my potatoes somewhere else. Good morning!"

"Goodness!" said Crooky to himself in dismay. "This is dreadful really. Where *is* that voice coming from? I've got something enchanted on me, there's no doubt of that. Well, I'll undress myself when I get home and see what it is. Maybe it's an enchanted spider or ladybird."

So when he got home the goblin carefully undressed himself. He shook out each of his clothes. He emptied his pockets. But he couldn't find a single thing that he thought might be magic. He didn't think of the button, of course! There it sat on the collar of the shirt, a little pearl button that looked exactly like the others!

"Well," said Crooky, dressing again, "it's a mystery. I can't find a single thing in my clothes that might be magic."

As he dressed he heard the doorbell

ring, and in came three customers. Crooky ran into the shop.

"Good morning," said Mrs Tibble. "I want six new-laid eggs."

"Certainly, madam," said Crooky. He put one old egg into the bag with the five new-laid ones, and handed them to Mrs Tibble.

"Cheat!" said the button. "One of those eggs is bad! Cheat!"

Crooky was so surprised that he dropped the bag of eggs. They all broke – and a dreadful smell came from one of them!

"What did I tell you?" said the button, and it laughed, just under Crooky's chin. "Pooh! What a smell!"

"I think I'll buy my eggs somewhere else," said Mrs Tibble in a huff.

"What can I do for *you*, madam?" asked Crooky, very red in the face, to his next customer, who was looking very nervous. It wasn't nice to hear a voice and not see who was speaking.

"I want some apples," said Miss Wriggle.

Crooky went to get them. He was just about to pop in a bad one, when the button spoke again:

"Now, naughty, naughty, naughty! That's a bad apple and you know it! Cheating again!"

Crooky hurriedly put a good apple into the bag instead. But when he turned round to give them to Miss Wriggle, she had gone – and so had the other customer too. They simply couldn't bear the button's remarks – they sounded too strange for anything.

Witch See-a-Lot popped her head in at the door just then, and grinned.

"Hallo!" she said – to the magic button, not to Crooky.

67

"Hallo!" said the button at once.

"How are you getting on?" asked the witch.

"Oh, having a fine old time," answered the button. "We're cheating hard, and I keep talking about it!"

Crooky stared down at his coat and wondered in despair where the voice came from. "*You've* done something magic!" he said to Witch See-a-Lot.

"I have!" grinned the witch. "But I shan't tell you what! Cheat all you like, Crooky – every one will know, and soon you'll have to shut up shop."

Well, Crooky didn't cheat at all after that. He really was too much afraid to. Maybe he'll learn one day that it's better to be honest – but if he doesn't, that enchanted button is still on his shirt, waiting to talk. Wouldn't I just love to hear it!

The
Magic Rubber

Once a very curious thing happened to Keith. He was walking home from school with his satchel full of school books. He remembered that he had half-finished a sum that rather puzzled him, and he sat down under the hedge and got out his exercise book.

He looked at the sum – and he saw that he had made a mistake in it. "Oh dear!" said Keith. "I'd better rub that out before I forget."

But he had left his rubber at school. What a nuisance! "Bother, bother, bother!" said Keith.

A funny little man peeped out of the hedge at Keith. He was a brownie with a very long beard and the brightest green eyes imaginable.

"Anything wrong?" he said politely.

"Well, nothing much," said Keith. "I was just wishing I had my rubber with me to rub out something, that's all."

"I'll lend you mine," said the brownie and put his hand in his pocket. He took out a rather marvellous rubber. It was gold one end, blue in the middle, and silver the other end. On it was stamped the brownie's name, TWINKLE.

"Just say, 'Rubber, rub out!' and it will rub out whatever mistake you have made and not leave a single mark," said the brownie. So Keith said, "Rubber, rub out!" and the rubber slipped out of his hand to his exercise book and rubbed out the mistake so smoothly that nobody could see where it had been.

"Excuse me a moment," said the brownie. "I think my telephone is ringing. I must just answer it."

Keith was rather astonished to think that a telephone should be in the hedge, but he could clearly hear a tiny, tinkling noise. And, whilst he waited for the brownie to come back, a naughty little thought came into his head.

"If I ran off home now, I could take this marvellous rubber with me, and show it to all the others! Wouldn't I feel grand with such a wonderful rubber?"

Well, it is always a pity when anyone does a mean thing. Keith didn't stop to think twice. He got up, flung his satchel over his shoulder, and ran off with the magic rubber safely in his pocket.

He got home panting and out of breath. Nobody followed him. He had the rubber for himself.

"I'll show it to everyone at school tomorrow," thought Keith. "I'd better not show it to Mother, because she will say I must take it back, if I tell her where I got it from."

That evening, when Keith did his homework, he had a fine time. Every time he made a mistake he said, "Rubber, rub out!" And it obeyed him

at once, and rubbed out every single mistake without leaving a mark. It rubbed out ink just as well as pencil, and Keith was able to write out his geography lesson most beautifully. In fact, he sometimes made a mistake on purpose so that he could get the rubber to rub it out.

"You seem to be a long time over your homework this evening, Keith," his mother called up to him. "Do hurry up. What are you doing?"

"Mother, I've written out my geography, and done six sums, and made out a list of French words, and I've drawn a map," said Keith, quite truthfully.

"Well, that's a lot," said Mother. "Come along down to supper now."

Keith put his rubber into his pocket and went downstairs, very pleased with his evening's work. He didn't say a word to Mother about the magic rubber, but he kept feeling it in his pocket. It really was marvellous, all silver and blue and gold.

The next morning Keith ran to school in a hurry. He didn't go the way he usually did because he didn't want to go by the hedge where the brownie lived. He went a different way. When he got to school he called his friends round him.

"Do you want to see something simply too marvellous for words?" he asked. "Well, look!"

Keith set out his exercise book with his sums so beautifully done, his geography lesson written out without a mistake, his nicely drawn map, and his list of French words.

"What do you think of my homework?" he asked. "Isn't it marvellous? Not a single mistake! I shall get top marks today."

74

"How do you do it so nicely?" asked Bill. "Usually you rub out about a hundred times, and leave messes all over your page. Mr Brown is always telling you about it."

"I'll show you how I managed it!" said Keith. "Look – I've got a magic rubber! Here it is."

"A magic rubber!" cried the boys. "How does it work? Where did you get it?"

"Well, when I say to it, 'Rubber, rub out!' it rubs out any mistake for me and doesn't leave a single mark," said Keith. As he showed his friends the rubber, and said, "Rubber, rub out," the rubber hopped from his hand and skipped to where Keith had spread out his homework books.

And my goodness me, in a second it had rubbed out all Keith's beautifully done homework! Yes – it rubbed out his geography lesson, his nice map, his list of French words, and all his sums! The pages shone quite bare and clean. Not a pencil or ink mark was on them.

Keith stared down in horror. "Oh, you silly, stupid rubber!" he cried. "What did you do that for? Now I've no

homework to show to Mr Brown, and I shall get into dreadful trouble."

He did get into dreadful trouble. You can guess that Mr Brown wouldn't believe Keith's tale about a magic rubber that had rubbed away all his beautiful homework. And when Keith put his hand into his pocket to get out the rubber, it wasn't there. No – it had slipped out and gone back to the brownie in the hedge. Nobody had noticed it hop-hop-hopping along the lane except a most surprised dog.

Keith had to lose his playtime and stay in after school to do all the homework again that the rubber had rubbed out. And this time his mistakes couldn't be rubbed out so beautifully, and he certainly didn't get top marks.

He is now trying to make up his mind to go and find that brownie again, and tell him he is sorry he ran off with his rubber, and he hopes it came back all right. I wonder if he will be brave enough to go and do that. Do you think he will?

The Pixie
in the Pond

Once upon a time there was a small pixie called Whistle. You can guess why he had that name – he was always whistling merrily! He lived with his mother and father in a little toadstool house not far from a big pond. It was a lonely house, for no other pixies lived near, and as white ducks swam on the pond there were no frogs or toads for Whistle to play with.

"I'm very lonely, Mother," Whistle said, a dozen times a day. "I wish I could play with the field-mice. They want to show me their tunnels under the roots of the oak tree."

"No, Whistle," said his mother firmly. "The last time you went to see a mouse's nest you got lost underground, and I had to pay three moles to go and look for you. You are *not* to play with field-mice."

"Well, can I play with the hedgehog then?" asked Whistle. "He is a good fellow for running about with me in the fields."

"Certainly not!" said his mother. "His prickles would tear your nice clothes to pieces. Now run out and play by yourself, Whistle, and don't worry me."

So Whistle went out by himself, looking very gloomy. It was dull having to play by himself, very dull. He shook his head when Tiny the field-mouse ran up to him and squeaked to him to come and play. He didn't go near the hedgehog when he saw him in the

ditch. Whistle was an obedient little pixie.

He ran off to the pond. He liked to watch the big dragonflies there. They were nearly as big as he was.

It was whilst he was watching the dragonflies that he saw a merry little head poking out of the water nearby, watching the dragonflies too! Whistle stared in surprise. He didn't know there was anybody else near, and here was a little pixie in the pond – a pixie about as small as himself, too!

"Hallo!" said Whistle. "Who are you?"

"I'm Splash, the water-pixie," said the little fellow, climbing out of the water and sitting beside Whistle. "I live in the pond with my father and mother.

We only came last week. I didn't think there was anyone for me to play with, and now I've found you. What luck!"

"Oh, Splash, I'm so pleased!" said Whistle. "My name is Whistle. We can play together every day. What shall we play at?"

"Come into the water and I'll teach you to swim," said Splash.

"But what about my clothes?" said Whistle. "They'll get wet."

"Well, they'll dry, won't they?" said Splash. "Come along! Mind that mud!"

But dear me, Whistle was so anxious to get into the water that he floundered right into the mud, and you should

81

have seen how he looked! He was black from head to foot!

"Oh dear!" said Whistle, in dismay. "Look at that! I'd better get out and dry myself, and then see if the mud will brush off. Come and sit by me, Splash, and I'll teach you to whistle."

So Splash sat by Whistle in the sun, and the pixie taught his friend to whistle loudly. By the time the dinner hour came, Splash could whistle like a blackbird! Whistle's clothes were dry, but the mud wouldn't brush off. It stuck to his clothes, and was all over his face and hands too. The two pixies said goodbye and each ran off to his dinner.

Oh dear! How cross Whistle's mother was when she saw his clothes! "You bad, naughty pixie!" she scolded. "You have been in the pond. Take off your clothes at once. You must have a hot bath."

"Oh, Mother, don't be angry with me," begged Whistle. "I have found a friend to play with. It is a water-pixie called Splash!"

"Indeed!" said his mother, pouring hot water into the tin bath. "Well, just remember this, Whistle – you are *not* to play with water-pixies at all! You will only get muddy and wet, and I won't have it!"

"But Mother!" cried Whistle, in dismay, "I do so like Splash! He is so nice. He wanted to teach me to swim."

"You'll drown before you learn to swim in that weedy pond," said his mother. "Now remember, Whistle, I forbid you to play with that water-pixie."

83

Whistle said no more. He knew it was no use, but he was very sad. It was hard to find a friend, and then not to be allowed to keep him.

That afternoon, Whistle stole down to the pond. Splash was there, sitting in a swing he had made of bent reed. He was whistling away, having a lovely time, eagerly waiting for Whistle.

"What's the matter?" he cried, when he saw the pixie's gloomy face.

"Mother was very cross about my muddy suit, and says I mustn't play with you," said Whistle sadly. "So I

came to tell you. After this I shan't come down to the pond, because if I do I might see you and play with you, and I don't want to upset my mother."

"Oh, bother!" said Splash, in dismay. "Just as we have found one another so nicely. It's too bad!"

"Goodbye, Splash," said Whistle. "I'm very, very sorry, but I must go."

Off he ran home; and just as he got there he met his father, who called to him.

"Whistle! How would you like to go for a sail on the pond this afternoon? I've got a fine little boat here that used to belong to a child."

"Ooh, how lovely!" said Whistle, looking at the toy boat, which was leaning up against the side of the toadstool house and was even bigger than the house itself!

"Mother! Where are you?" called Whistle, in excitement. "Are you coming for a sail, too?"

"Yes!" said his mother. So in a short time the little family set off to the pond,

Whistle and his father carrying the ship, and his mother running behind.

They set the boat on the water, and then they all got in.

It was a windy day. The wind filled the little white sail and the ship blew into the middle of the pond. What fun it was! Whistle's father guided the boat along and Whistle leaned so far over that he lost his balance! Splash! Into the water he went head-first!

"Oh! Oh! Save him! He can't swim!" cried Whistle's mother in dismay. "Oh, Whistle, Whistle! Quick, turn the boat

about and save Whistle!"

But just then the wind blew so hard that the ship simply tore across the pond and left Whistle struggling in the water. Poor little pixie – he couldn't swim, and he was in great trouble.

But suddenly up swam Splash, the water-pixie. He had watched the boat

87

setting sail, and had kept by it all the way, though the others hadn't seen him. As soon as he saw his friend fall into the water he swam up to him, and catching hold of him under the arms, he swam with him to the boat.

"Oh, you brave little fellow!" said Whistle's father, as he pulled the two of them into the boat. "You have saved Whistle! He might have drowned! Who are you?"

"I am Splash, the water-pixie," said

Splash. "I live in the pond. I would very much like to be friends with Whistle and teach him to swim. He has taught me to whistle like a blackbird, and my mother is very pleased. I should like to do something for him in return."

"Oh, you are the bravest little pixie I have ever seen!" cried Whistle's mother, as she sat hugging Whistle to her. "Please be friends with Whistle. He must certainly learn to swim. I will make him a little bathing suit, and then it won't matter if he gets wet or muddy."

"Oh, Mother, how lovely!" cried Whistle, in delight. "I told Splash this afternoon that I could never see him again, and I said goodbye to him, because you said I wasn't to play with him – and now he is to be my friend after all!"

"You deserve it, for you're a good, obedient little pixie," said his father. "Now you'd better bring your friend home to tea with you, if Mother has enough cake!"

"Oh yes, I made treacle buns this morning," said Whistle's mother, "and there is some new blackberry jam too. Ask your mother if you can come, Splash!"

Splash jumped into the water and swam to his cosy little home in the reeds. In a moment or two, three pixies popped their heads out of the water – for Splash had brought his father and mother.

"Thank you for the invitation," said Splash's pretty little pixie mother. "He will be most delighted to come. I am just going to brush his hair. Perhaps you will all come to tea with us tomorrow? We should love to have you."

So all the pixies became friends, and now Splash and Whistle play together all day long, and Whistle can swim just as well as Splash can; and as for Splash's whistling, well you should just hear it! The two pixies sound like a cage full of canaries!

91

Too Good
to Be True

Binkie and Tigger were cross. Their Aunt Work-a-Lot had just turned them out of her house without even a slice of bread and butter for their dinner!

"Mean old thing! Just because we didn't dig up her garden for her!" said Binkie.

"And she said we hadn't swept the backyard," grumbled Tigger. "What's the matter with the backyard? Why can't it be dirty? All this fuss about being clean and tidy and working hard for a living!"

They were walking beside the river. It flowed calmly along in the sunshine and looked very peaceful.

"It's a pity we were born pixies," said Binkie gloomily. "Why couldn't we be a river? Just flowing along because it can't do anything else. No cross aunt to make it rush here and there and do silly jobs."

"I'm hot," said Tigger, and he flung himself down beside the water. "Here's a nice, warm, cosy little cove, Binkie. Let's bask in the sun."

"We're supposed to go and fetch potatoes from the farm," said Binkie, but he sat down beside Tigger all the same. "Ah-h-h-h! How nice to be somewhere that Aunt Work-a-Lot isn't."

They took off their shoes and stockings and put their feet into the warm water. Then they lay back, tipped

their pixie caps over their ears, and talked lazily.

"What we want is some good luck," said Binkie. "Just a little bit of good luck – like finding a pound – or some wonderful spell."

"I could do with finding some dinner," said Tigger dolefully. "I had hardly any breakfast. I'm terribly hungry. We are very badly treated, Binkie. We deserve a great *big* piece of good luck, not a little bit."

Now a good way up the river was Mr Hey-There, the goblin. He had rowed all the way up against the stream, panting and puffing. He knew of a nice place to fish. He had brought a very fine lunch with him, a rubber sheet to sit on, a big umbrella in case it rained, and two fat books to read if the fish didn't bite.

Aha! Mr Hey-There meant to have a very nice day indeed – plenty to eat, plenty to drink, plenty of fish to catch (he hoped) and books to read if he didn't.

He came to the place he wanted. He flung the boat's rope over a tree stump and jumped out. He took with him his fishing-rod, meaning to get it ready first of all.

Then he grunted crossly. Three cows were staring at him from just nearby.

He didn't like cows. He didn't like anything that came and breathed down his neck whilst he was fishing. It frightened the fish in the water, and it made him feel very uncomfortable. He was always afraid that the horse or cow breathing over him might begin to nibble his hair, thinking it was grass.

95

So what did Mr Hey-There do but address the cows very sternly and tell them to go away at once.

"Hey, there!" he shouted. "Shoo, go away!"

The cows chewed hard as they stood staring at him and didn't budge an inch. So Mr Hey-There had to chase them. First he chased one cow away, and then another, and then the third. By the time he had chased the third away to the other end of the field, the first two had come back to his fishing rod and were staring at it as if they thought it might be good to eat.

So Mr Hey-There had to begin his chasing all over again. It took a lot of time and was most annoying. But the most annoying thing of all was still to come.

When at last he had got all the cows at the other end of the field, and was back where he had left the boat, there was no boat!

It had gone. It simply wasn't there – nor were his lunch, his books, his umbrella or his rubber sheet to sit on. Only his fishing-rod waiting for him.

Mr Hey-There stamped so hard on the bank in his rage that all the fish in the water nearby rushed off as if sharks were after them.

"It's gone!" raged Mr Hey-There. "Floated off down the river by itself.

97

Now I've got to walk miles down the bank to find it! What a day! All because of those three cows that came to breathe down my neck."

The boat had indeed gone off by itself. The rope hadn't been made fast to the tree stump and had simply slid into the water. So the river had taken the boat, and it was now floating back gently and peacefully all the way it had come.

In fact, it floated right down to the little cove where Binkie and Tigger were lying, with their feet dabbling in

the warm water. The current took the
boat into the cove, and it bobbed over to
the lazy pixies. They didn't see it
because they were lying on their backs
in the sun.

They were still talking about good
luck. "Some people have it and some
people don't," Binkie was saying. "It's
not fair."

"Aunt Work-a-Lot always says that
good luck comes to people who work for
it," said Tigger gloomily. "Oh, Binkie,
wouldn't it be nice to have a great big
bit of good luck – something like a wish
that came true?"

"If I had a wish, I'd wish for a jolly
big lunch right away this very minute,"
said Binkie.

Just at that moment the boat
bumped gently against his toes. He
thought it was Tigger's feet bumping
him. "Don't," he said.

"Don't what?" asked Tigger in
surprise.

"Don't push my feet," said Binkie.

"I'm not," said Tigger, and just then

the boat pushed quite hard against all their four feet in the water.

"Don't!" they both said at once. "Leave my feet alone!"

Tigger sat up crossly. He suddenly saw the boat. "I say, Binkie! Look here! It's a boat!"

Binkie sat up, too. "A boat! Golly! There's no one in it. Oh, Tigger, do you think it's been sent to us?"

"Who would have sent it?" said Tigger. "Don't be silly."

"It might be a bit of good luck suddenly arrived!" said Binkie. "Boats never come without people in them.

This must be a magic boat, a good luck boat! A boat full of good things for us! Oh, Tigger!"

Tigger pulled the boat into the cove. "My goodness – look at this basket of food!"

"Oh!" said Binkie, overcome with joy. "My wish has come true. Don't you remember how I wished for a jolly good lunch, Tigger? I'll share it with you."

"You'll *share* it?" said Tigger indignantly. "I should think you will! It isn't yours. It's *ours*. The boat came to both of us."

"All right, all right," said Binkie, and he took the big basket of food out of the boat. There were two ginger-beer bottles beside it.

"Look at those!" Tigger said joyfully. "Our favourite drink!"

"What else is there?" asked Binkie. "A rubber sheet for us to sit on. How very thoughtful! I did think the grass was a bit damp, didn't you, Tigger? And look – two lovely, fat storybooks to read when we've finished our dinner!"

"And even an umbrella in case it rains," said Tigger. "It might quite easily rain. Oh, Binkie, it looks as if somebody has planned a really lovely day for us – plenty to eat and drink, a ground sheet to sit on, books to read, and an umbrella in case it rains. This must be the big piece of good luck we've been talking about."

They took everything out of the boat. They spread the ground sheet on the grass, poked the umbrella down a rabbit-hole to keep it safe, put the books beside them, and opened the dinner-basket.

"Chicken sandwiches! My favourite!" said Binkie in delight.

"Egg and tomato! My favourite!" said

Tigger joyfully. "Plum cake! Currant buns! Chocolate biscuits! Oh, Binkie, if this is the lunch you wished us, I must say you know what to wish for!"

They ate every single thing in the basket. They drank the ginger-beer out of the bottles. They were just going to settle down in the sunshine to read their books when two cows came down to the water.

"Go away, cows," said Binkie. "Go to another part of the river to drink. This is our bit. Oh, look, Tigger, that cow is eating the paper bags. Shoo, cow, shoo!"

The cows wouldn't shoo, so the two pixies got up to chase them away. They ran up the river bank, shouting and yelling. The cows lumbered slowly away.

A little way up the river bank Binkie and Tigger met an angry-looking goblin. It was Mr Hey-There, still looking for his boat. He called to Binkie and Tigger.

"Hey, there! I want to ask you something."

Binkie and Tigger didn't like goblins. They turned away and began to walk back to their cove. Mr Hey-There put his two heavy hands on their shoulders.

"Now then! You'll answer my questions if I want you to."

"Certainly, sir," said Binkie in a fright, not liking the feel of the goblin's knobbly fingers at all.

"I'm looking for a boat," said Mr Hey-There.

"Oh,"said Tigger at once. "We've got one we can hire out to you, goblin."

"I'm not looking for one to hire," said Mr Hey-There. "I'm looking for my own boat. And for my dinner that was in it."

"D-d-d-dinner?" stammered Binkie, feeling rather faint all of a sudden.

"Yes, dinner," said Mr Hey-There crossly. "Have you never heard of dinner before? My dinner was chicken sandwiches, egg and tomato sandwiches, plum cake, currant buns, chocolate biscuits ..."

"Was – was it really?" said Tigger, stammering too.

"What's the matter with you two pixies?" said Mr Hey-There. "Stammering and stuttering and looking so silly! Have you seen my boat?"

"Well – we don't know if it was *your* boat," began Binkie, wishing he was a hundred miles away. "If you'd take your knobbly hands off our shoulders, goblin, we could lead you to where we know there is a boat."

"You'll lead me to it *with* my hands on your shoulders," said Mr Hey-There, beginning to feel there was something odd about all this. "Now – quick march!"

And quick-march it had to be! Down to the cover went all three – and then Mr Hey-There stood and gazed at his empty dinner-basket, his books, his ginger-beer bottles and his rubber sheet. He saw the handle of his umbrella sticking out of the rabbit-hole. He saw his boat, still nosing into the little cove.

"You've eaten my dinner! How dare you! You little thieves! You greedy, dishonest robbers! Now, you get into that boat and row me all the way upstream to the police-station. Go on – get in. Bring that umbrella. It will do to poke you with when you row too slowly!" roared Mr Hey-There.

And into that boat Binkie and Tigger had to climb, and row it slowly for a whole mile up the river to where the little stone police station stood. How they panted and puffed! Mr Hey-There

wouldn't allow them even a minute's rest. If one or other of them stopped rowing he would poke them with the end of his umbrella.

"Thieves and robbers," he kept saying. He wouldn't listen to a word that Binkie and Tigger said.

"We thought it was a wish come true when your boat came," cried Binkie. "We thought it was a piece of good luck. We did really."

It was no good saying anything at all. Mr Hey-There wouldn't listen. The big policeman wouldn't listen. And when they got Aunt Work-a-Lot to come

along, she wouldn't listen either.

"They are just a couple of lazy rascals," she said. "They want a good telling off each, and some hard work to do. That would put them right."

Well, they got the telling off, and Mr Hey-There gave them some hard work, too. He said they must row him home and spend a whole week with him, digging up his garden. That would pay for the dinner they had eaten.

"I shall never make a wish again,"

said poor Binkie at the end of that dreadful week.

"I shall never hope for good luck again," said Tigger.

"But oh – wasn't it *lovely* when we sat up on the river bank and saw that boat full of good things?" sighed Binkie.

Then back they had to go to Aunt Work-a-Lot. They had had to work so very hard at Mr Hey-There's that their aunt's little jobs seemed quite easy to do. She was pleased with them.

"You've quite changed for the better!" she said. "Well, if you do that, so will I! I'll make you pineapple jelly with cherries and whipped cream on top for supper!"

Oooooh! Binkie and Tigger beamed at one another. What a bit of good luck. Perhaps things weren't going to be so bad after all!

Porridge
Town

There was once a little boy called James, who was very messy with his porridge at breakfast-time. He liked to stir it round and round in his plate, and then it always went over the edge on to the cloth.

"James! You've dirtied the clean tablecloth again!" cried his mother almost every day. "Oh dear, if only you would try and eat your porridge up properly instead of getting it on the floor and on the table!"

After James had finished his breakfast each morning, Mummy had to take a cloth and wipe up porridge spots on the carpet, dropped off James's spoon, and she had to wipe up plenty of messes on the cloth as well.

One morning Mummy was very cross with James because he had made a bigger mess than usual.

"Now, James! I am going to get a cloth to wipe up that mess," she said, "and if your porridge is not finished by the time I come back, you shall not have your nice boiled egg this morning, and you will have to sit in the corner and think about porridge for half an hour!"

Mummy went to get a cloth. Did James eat his porridge up quickly as soon as she had gone? No, he did not! He sat there, dreaming, looking out of the window, stirring his porridge and making some more slop over the edge of his plate. He really was a most annoying child.

Then he heard Mummy coming back, and he remembered what she had said. No egg – and half an hour in the corner if he hadn't emptied his plate of porridge! Well, there certainly wasn't time to eat it. Whatever was he to do?

You will never guess what that

naughty boy did! He took up his plate, turned it upside down out of the window, and emptied all his porridge into the garden.

He heard an angry yell from below the window, but he hadn't time to look out and see what had happened because Mummy came back. She took a look at his plate and said, "Oh, so you have managed to eat up your porridge quickly for once. And a good thing too!"

Naughty James didn't say a word. He watched Mummy wipe up the mess he had made, and then he began to eat his egg, wondering who had yelled like that in the garden.

He soon found out when he went to play on the lawn. A fierce little brownie-man ran out from under the lilac-bush and caught hold of him.

"Was it you who poured porridge all over me?" he cried angrily. "Look at me! It's all over my hair and down my neck! You nasty, horrid boy!"

James looked at the angry little man, and he began to laugh. The brownie had porridge all over his hat and down his neck. He really did look funny.

"Oh! So instead of begging my pardon you think you'll laugh at me, do you!" shouted the brownie, getting crosser and crosser. "Well, my boy, you just come along with me to Porridge Town! It isn't very far, and maybe you will see then what it is like to have porridge when you don't want it!"

Then, to James's surprise and dismay, he dragged him to the gate, whisked him down a path, and through a strange gate that James knew he had never seen before – and before he could say anything, there he was in a crooked little town, with tumbledown houses, twisty chimneys, and a crowd of little folk going about their shopping.

"This is Porridge Town," said the

brownie with a grin. "Have a good time, nasty little boy!"

James didn't like the look of Porridge Town at all. He wandered along by himself, and came to a seat by the road. He sat down on it. Presently a bus came along, and splashed through a big puddle – and the puddle splashed all over poor James.

And when he looked down to see if his suit had been messed, he found that he was all over porridge!

Yes – all the puddles in the road were full of porridge instead of water. It was most disgusting! Poor James tried to wipe the porridge off himself, but his hanky soon got wet and sticky.

He got up and went on again. He saw some lovely buns in a baker's shop, and he wondered if he had a penny. Yes – he had. So into the shop he went and bought a penny bun.

But, dear me, when he bit into it, what a surprise! The inside was full of porridge that squirted out all over James! Some went down his neck and some went on to his chest.

The little folk who were passing thought it was a great joke, and they laughed and laughed at him. James was angry and ran away. He fell down – and of course he fell into a porridge puddle! He did hate that.

A little old woman came out of a nearby cottage and helped him up. "Come and rest in my cottage for a minute and I'll tie up your knee," she said.

So into her house went James and sat down on a nice, fat, soft cushion. And, do you know, it burst under him, and goodness gracious, will you believe it, it was full of porridge!

Well, it is horrid enough to fall down in a porridge puddle, but it is even worse to *sit* in porridge! James got up in a hurry and went out of the cottage at a run. He simply couldn't bear the idea of sitting down in another chair there.

Not far off was a big apple tree and on it were some rosy, ripe apples. It was not the time of year for apples and James was most surprised. He thought he would go and sit under the tree and maybe an apple would fall down by him, and he could eat it.

Well, the apples were very ripe and they did fall down. But they were not like ordinary apples. Oh no!

One fell on to James's head and burst at once – and as you can guess, it was

full of porridge. In fact, it was a porridge-apple! Another one fell down and burst on his shoulder, sending wet porridge down his neck. A third apple fell on his hand, and covered it with porridge too – hot porridge this time, so that James was burnt and sprang up with a shout of pain!

He ran away from that peculiar tree. He ran and he ran. He didn't know where he was going to, but he meant to get away from Porridge Town. He ran fast. It seemed to him as if he ran for miles. And after a while he found himself on a path in a garden, rushing along at top speed.

He bumped into someone. "What's the hurry?" cried a voice.

"I want to get home!" cried James. "Tell me the way!"

Then he looked up and saw – his mother! She *was* astonished.

"You *are* at home!" she said. "Fancy galloping along like this at sixty miles an hour to get home when you are in your own garden. Really, James!"

"Am I in my own garden? How funny!" cried James. "I've been all the way to Porridge Town and back, Mother."

"Well, I hope you didn't make as much mess there as you did at breakfast this morning!" said his mother. James looked down at himself – and to his surprise he was quite clean. He hadn't a scrap of porridge on him. Could he possibly have imagined it all?

But, dear me, when he put his hands into his pockets, what a shock he got! They were full of porridge – hot porridge, too! That was the last trick one of the little folk in Porridge Town had managed to play on him. Poor James! He didn't say a word to his mother but hurried off to the bathroom. He turned his pockets inside out and tried his best to sponge out the porridge. And he made up his mind about something.

"I shall eat up my porridge in the morning and not make a single mess!" he said to himself. "Oh dear – I really don't think I could *BEAR* to see a porridge spot on the cloth again!"

Do you make messes? What! You do? Come along to Porridge Town then, and we'll see what happens!

Poor Old
Lazy-Bones

"Bother!" said old Dame Look-Sharp. "Oh, bother, bother!"

"What's the matter?" asked Lazy-Bones, her little servant.

"Well, I'm in the middle of making a most important spell, and I haven't got something I need for it," said Dame Look-Sharp.

"What's that?" asked Lazy-Bones. "I hope it isn't something I've got to fetch. I'm tired."

"You aren't tired, you're just lazy," said Dame Look-Sharp. "I've forgotten to get a seashell. This spell needs the sound of the sea that you hear inside a big seashell. And I've forgotten the shell. Run up to Mister Keep-All's shop, Lazy-Bones, and buy one for me."

"Oh, dear, Keep-All's shop is a mile away," groaned Lazy-Bones. "I don't want to go."

"You go at once, and look sharp!" said old Dame Look-Sharp crossly. "You want a good scolding, I can see."

Lazy-Bones got up, groaning. He put on his hat and went up the hill that led to Mister Keep-All's shop. But on the way he suddenly thought of something.

124

"Oh! I know! Dame Goody has a big seashell in her house! I've seen it there heaps of times. Her house is only half as far as Mister Keep-All's shop. I'll go there and borrow her shell. I can easily take it back when Dame Look-Sharp has finished with it." Lazy-Bones was pleased. He made his way to Dame Goody's and knocked at her door.

"Well, Lazy-Bones, what do you want?" asked Dame Goody.

"Please, Dame Goody, would you lend me that big seashell?" asked Lazy-Bones. "I'll bring it back tomorrow."

"I'll lend it to you with pleasure, if you will do something for me," said Dame Goody.

"What?" asked Lazy-Bones. "I'm rather tired!"

"You're lazy, not tired," said Dame Goody. "Now listen – you shall have the shell if you will go to the Bee-Woman, and ask her for a pot of honey for me. She promised me one a long time ago."

"Oh, dear. The Bee-Woman lives a long way away," said Lazy-Bones. Then

125

he caught sight of the shell on the side table, and nodded his head. "All right. I'll go."

Off he went to the Bee-Woman's cottage. He had to go down the hill again, and up on to the common where the heather grew. The bees took the honey from the heather, and put it into the Bee-Woman's hives. Then the Bee-Woman put it into pots and jars. It was clear and sweet and golden.

Lazy-Bones knocked at the Bee-Woman's door. "Come round the back!" called a voice. "I'm hanging out my washing."

So Lazy-Bones went round the back.

The Bee-Woman was surprised to see him.

"Please," said Lazy-Bones, "Dame Goody says will you let her have the pot of honey you promised her a long time ago?"

"Dear me! I'd forgotten all about it!" said the Bee-Woman. "I don't believe I've a small pot left – only my very big ones, and I can't spare one of those."

"Please let me have some honey for her," said Lazy-Bones, thinking that he wouldn't get the seashell if he didn't take back the honey to Dame Goody.

"Well, listen – you run along to my brother, Old Man Mardy," said the Bee-Woman. "He may have a small jar that will do. Borrow it for me and tell him I'll let him have a jar as soon as I get some more."

Lazy-Bones looked sulky as he set off for Old Man Mardy's. He didn't like the cross old fellow. And besides, he was doing far too many errands for his liking! What a lot to do for a stupid seashell!

He came to Old Man Mardy's and banged at the door very loudly, because Old Man Mardy was deaf.

Old Man Mardy came to the door in a rage. "Now, what's the matter, what's the matter, banging the door down like that?" he shouted. "Anyone would think I am deaf."

"Well, I thought you were," said Lazy-Bones, in surprise. Old Man Mardy didn't hear him.

"Speak up, speak up!" he said. "You youngsters mumble so much now."

"I said, 'I thought you *were* deaf!'" said Lazy-Bones.

Old Man Mardy frowned till his eyebrows touched his nose.

"Deaf! I'd like to know who said I was deaf!" he said. "And don't shout at me like that. I can hear quite well."

"Oh," said Lazy-Bones, not knowing whether to shout or to whisper now.

"Well?" said Old Man Mardy. "Am I to stand here all day waiting for you to tell me what you have come for? Speak up and tell me."

129

"The Bee-Woman says, please will you let her have a small jar to put honey in," said Lazy-Bones, loudly.

"A small car to put money in?" said Old Man Mardy, looking surprised.

"No – a small *jar* to put *honey* in," said Lazy-Bones. Old Man Mardy put his hands to his ears and frowned again.

"Don't shout so," he said. "I heard you. What does the Bee-Woman want with a small star to put Bunny in? I didn't know she kept rabbits."

Lazy-Bones began to feel that Old Man Mardy was being stupid on purpose. He tried again, and this time the old fellow heard.

"Oh – a small jar to put honey in," he said. "Well, why didn't you say that before, instead of talking about cars to put money in, and rabbits?"

"I *did* say it before," said Lazy-Bones, getting cross.

"Now my boy – if you are rude to me I'll turn you upside down and shake you as if I was emptying a sack," said Old Man Mardy. Once the old man had done this to a rude boy, and Lazy-Bones didn't want it to happen to him. So he became very polite.

"I don't know quite where the jar is," said Old Man Mardy. "It will take me a few minutes to look for it. Whilst I am doing that, you run along to the Clever Goblin, and ask him to lend me this morning's newspaper."

"I don't want to. I'm tired," said Lazy-Bones.

"You're not tired, you're lazy," said

131

Old Man Mardy. "You go along, or I won't get the jar for you."

So grumbling as loudly as he dared, Lazy-Bones set off for the Clever Goblin's cave. He was a bit afraid of the Clever Goblin, because the Goblin didn't like lazy people. He was always hard at work himself, doing very peculiar things, and he thought everyone else ought to be busy, too.

Lazy-Bones came to the Goblin's cave. But there was nobody there. "Oh, bother, bother!" he said. Then he saw

the newspaper lying on a chair inside the cave.

"It won't matter if I take it," he thought. So he went in and took up the newspaper. But a loud voice roared at him at once.

"What are you doing with my paper?"

Lazy-Bones dropped the paper as if it was burning him.

"Old M-M-Man M-M-Mardy asked me to b-b-borrow it from you," he stammered. "Where are you, Clever Goblin? I can't see you."

"I've turned myself into a skipping rope, just to see if I could," said the voice of the Goblin, and then Lazy-Bones saw a skipping rope hanging over a chair wriggling at him. He couldn't help thinking it was a silly idea to turn into a skipping rope but he didn't like to say so.

"Well, can I have the paper?" asked Lazy-Bones, staring at the skipping rope.

"First of all, try skipping a bit with me, will you?" asked the Clever Goblin, and the rope jumped off the chair and hopped to Lazy-Bones.

"Come on – take my handles – and skip forwards one hundred times, backwards one hundred times, and then forwards and backwards, crossing your arms one hundred times."

"I couldn't, I couldn't," said Lazy-Bones, in horror. "Why, I'm tired already, and I should hardly be able to walk home if I did that."

"You're not tired, you're only lazy," said the Goblin, and he tapped Lazy-Bones' hands hard with the handles of the skipping rope. There was nothing for it but to begin skipping. The Clever Goblin was not very good-tempered, and Lazy-Bones did not want to be

turned into a rope, or a ball or anything
that came into the Goblin's head. So he
began skipping.

He skipped and he skipped. He had
to, because the rope turned itself and
slashed his ankles smartly if he didn't
jump. Poor Lazy-Bones sank to the
floor when he had finished. The Clever
Goblin laughed.

"Ha! That made you work a bit! You
can take the paper now. If you come

135

tomorrow, I daresay I shall be a ball and you can bounce me."

Lazy-Bones staggered out, making up his mind that he would never go near the Clever Goblin again. He went back to Old Man Mardy and gave him the paper.

"Here's the jar," said the old man. "My word – what's the matter with your legs? They *are* shaky!"

Lazy-Bones didn't answer. He staggered on till he came to the Bee-Woman's, and he gave her the jar.

"What's the matter with your legs?" she said.

"Nothing. I've been skipping, that's all," said Lazy-Bones, who knew that the Bee-Woman would laugh if she knew what he had had to do.

"Well, here's the honey for Dame Goody," said the Bee-Woman. "Now, go carefully, and don't drop it, or my bees will come after you!"

Lazy-Bones couldn't help going carefully, because his legs were too tired to go quickly. He went on and on, groaning to himself, till he came to Dame Goody's. He went in and set the honey down on the table.

"Thank you," said Dame Goody. "Dear me, what's the matter with your legs, Lazy-Bones?"

"I've been skipping," said Lazy-Bones, wishing that people wouldn't ask so many questions.

"Skipping! You naughty boy!" said

Dame Goody. "So that's what you were doing – and all the time poor Dame Look-Sharp was waiting and waiting for the seashell!"

"Can I take it now?" said Lazy-Bones, suddenly thinking that he had been gone a very long time and remembering that Dame Look-Sharp did not like to be kept waiting. He looked at the side table – but to his horror the shell was not there!

"Dame Look-Sharp came to borrow it," said Dame Goody. "She said she had sent you to buy one at old Mister Keep-All's, but you were such a long time she couldn't wait any more – and she

remembered I had a seashell in my house and came to borrow it. I'm afraid you will get into trouble when you get back!"

Lazy-Bones was frightened. He looked at Dame Goody. "I don't want to go back," he said. "Do *you* want a good servant, Dame Goody?"

"I don't want a lazy-bones like you," said Dame Goody, and she shooed poor Lazy-Bones out of the house. He went crying down the hill.

"And where have *you* been?" cried Dame Look-Sharp, in a temper.

"I went to Dame Goody's to borrow her shell because it was such a long way to Keep-All's shop," he wept. "And she sent me to the Bee-Woman – and the Bee-Woman sent me to Old Man Mardy's – and he sent me to the Clever Goblin's – and he made me skip hundreds of times because he had turned himself into a rope – and now I am dreadfully tired!"

"Serves you right!" said Dame Look-Sharp, and she began to laugh. "If you had gone straight to Mister Keep-All's, you wouldn't have had to walk nearly so far as you have done, and you wouldn't have had to skip, either. You've had to do more because you were lazy than you would have done if you had been working. Serves you right! You try and remember that another time, Lazy-Bones!"

But he won't, you know. He's sure to do something just as silly another time!

The Very
Strange Pool

Now once upon a time Shiny-One the gnome had to take a heavy mirror to Dame Pretty. It was a very large looking-glass indeed, bigger than Shiny-One himself, so it made him puff and pant, as you can imagine.

When he got to the middle of Cuckoo Wood he felt that he really *must* have a rest. So he laid the mirror flat on the ground, with the bracken and grass peeping into it, and went to lean against a tree a little way off. And he fell fast asleep.

Now along that way came little Peep and Pry, the two pixies who lived at the edge of the wood. They were always peeping and prying into things that were no business of theirs – so you can

guess they were most astonished to see a big flat shining thing in the middle of the wood!

"Look at that!" said Peep. "A new pool!"

"A lovely, shiny pool!" said Pry. They both ran to it – and indeed, the mirror did look exactly like a shining pool of clear water, for it reflected the grass, the bracken, the trees, and the sky exactly as a sheet of water does.

"I wonder how a pool suddenly came here," said Peep. "It's really rather extraordinary. There was never one here before."

"It hasn't been raining," said Pry. "I just can't understand it. Do you suppose it is a magic pool, Peep?"

"Yes – perhaps it is," said Peep.

"Peep – shall we take a little drink from it, in case it's a wishing-pool?" whispered Pry.

"Well – do you think we'd better?" said Peep. "Suppose it belongs to somebody?"

"They'll never know," said naughty Pry. "Come on – let's scoop a little water up in our hands and drink it. We'll wish at the same time."

Peep put his hand down to the mirror – but, of course, all he felt was something hard, and not soft water! He stared in astonishment.

"The pool's frozen!" he said. "Look – there's no water – only ice."

"Well, that *shows* it's magic!" said Pry at once. "That just shows it is! How could water freeze on a warm autumn day like this? It's impossible."

"I think you're right," said Peep in excitement. "Yes, I really think you are. A pool that is frozen hard on a warm day *must* be magic! Whoever it belongs to must have frozen it so that nobody could take a drink and wish."

"Ah – but we can manage to trick the owner!" said Pry in a whisper. "We can break the ice, Peep – and drink the water below! Can't we?"

"Of course!" said Peep. "Come on – let's break it, and drink quickly, before anyone comes."

So they took stones and banged the pool hard – crack! The mirror broke into little pieces – and to the pixies'

great astonishment there was no water underneath!

"Stranger and stranger!" said Peep. "I wish there was somebody we could tell this to."

Then they saw Shiny-One the gnome, not very far off, just waking up. They ran to him.

"I say, there's a magic pool over there!"

"We knew it was magic because it was frozen hard."

"So we cracked the ice to get a drink of the water underneath – but there wasn't any! Did you ever know such magic?"

"What nonsense are you talking?" said Shiny-One crossly. He knew Peep and Pry well and didn't like the way they poked their noses into things that had nothing to do with them. "A magic pool – frozen on a day like this! Rubbish!"

Peep and Pry took him to the pool – and Shiny-One stared down in horror at his poor broken mirror.

"My mirror!" he said. "The one I was

selling to Dame Pretty. Look what you've done, with your silly interfering ways – smashed that beautiful big mirror! You bad pixies! How much money have you got in your pockets? You'll have to pay for that mirror."

Peep and Pry tried to run away – but Shiny-One caught hold of them both. He turned them upside down and shook them well. All their money rolled out of their pockets.

"Thank you," said Shiny-One, and he turned the pixies the right way up. "Thank you! Just enough to pay for a new mirror, I think. Now run off before I think of chasing you all the way home."

Peep and Pry ran off, crying. Shiny-One dug a hole with a stick and buried all the bits of broken mirror, so that nobody's feet would get cut.

As for Peep and Pry, they couldn't buy sweets for four weeks, because all their money had gone – so maybe they won't go poking their noses about quite so much another time!

The Tale of
Chuckle and Ho

When Chuckle and Ho came to
Toadstool Town nobody liked them
very much. They were cheeky, lazy
pixies, and they played such a lot of silly
tricks that the Toadstool Folk soon
became very tired of them.

"They want a good scolding," said
High-Hat, the chief person in Toadstool
Town. "Send them to me, please."

So Chuckle and Ho were brought
before High-Hat, and to their great
surprise and horror they were well and
truly told-off.

"You look surprised," said High-Hat,
when he had finished. "You shouldn't
be surprised at all. People who come
here and don't work are always
punished. You must go away from

Toadstool Town by tomorrow unless you get some work to do."

With tears running down their cheeks the two pixies went away, angry and upset.

"To think that this should happen to *us*!" said Chuckle, rubbing his eyes. "What have we done to deserve it?"

"Nothing at all," said Ho. "We hid round corners and jumped out at people, but that's nothing. And we chased Dame Ricky's hens a bit, but who minds about that?"

"And we knocked at High-Hat's door every morning and ran away," said Chuckle. "But that's only a bit of fun. Horrid old High-Hat!"

"And horrid people of Toadstool Town!" said Ho, seeing everyone grinning when they passed them.

"Look at them laughing at us. I wish we could pay them back for their horridness."

"Well, let's," said Chuckle, cheering up a bit. "We've got plenty of brains when we like to use them. Let's think of a way to pay them back."

Old Mister Bent passed them just then. He coughed as he went, and he held in his hand an empty bottle, with "Cough Mixture" written on it. He went into Mister Scales the chemist's.

"Old Scales must make a lot of money selling medicine," said Ho. Then an idea came into his head and he clutched Chuckle's arm so suddenly that he made him jump. "Chuckle, I've got an idea! Quick, come under this bush and I'll whisper it."

They crept under the bush and Ho whispered into Chuckle's ear: "Listen! Can't we get a spell to make people cough – and then sell Magic Cough Medicine somewhere nearby? It would be simply wonderful. We should be doing work – we should be making

money – and we should be punishing the folk of Toadstool Town for being horrid to us!"

"How?" asked Chuckle.

"Well – we'll put a Blue-Nose Spell into the cough medicine," said Ho. "See? Whoever drinks our medicine will get a bright-blue nose. Think how upset everyone will be!"

Chuckle began to laugh. "It's a wonderful plan!" he said. "Let's think how to work it."

So they thought. "We'll take two toadstool houses next door to one another," said Ho. "And when somebody comes by I'll sweep my doorstep hard – and I'll put a Coughing Spell into the dust I sweep."

"Then whoever comes by will begin to cough when they get covered in your dust," said Chuckle. "And they will come next to *my* toadstool, and I shall be sitting outside with a row of bottles on a table, labelled 'Magic Cough Medicine'. And they will be sure to buy a bottle to stop their coughs, so we shall make a lot of money."

"There will be a Blue-Nose Spell in each bottle – and the very next day the people who have drunk the medicine

152

will wake up to find their noses are a bright blue!" said Ho. He rolled over and over and laughed till he frightened all the birds out of the bush he was under.

The two pixies set to work. Ho went off to his grandmother and bought a Coughing Spell and a Blue-Nose Spell. "They are for the Wizard of the Blue Mountains," he told his granny, most untruthfully. "He has sent me for them. So give me nice strong spells, Granny."

He took the spells back to Chuckle.
The Coughing Spell was blue powder.
The Blue-Nose Spell was blue pills that
had to be dissolved in water before
being used.

"Here you are!" said Ho, joyfully.
"Now we can start. Let's go and rent
those two toadstool houses over there,
at the side of the High Street. Lots of
people will pass by there."

Soon they were in the two houses. Ho
was in the garden stretching between
them. He collected a pailful of dust, and
mixed the blue Coughing Powder with
it. Then he spread a little of the dust on

154

his doorstep, ready to sweep it up when anyone came by.

Chuckle made the Magic Cough Medicine. He decided to make it as nasty as possible, to punish the folk of Toadstool Town for laughing at him when he had been ticked off. So he put into it all the horrid, bitter things he could think of, and then added the Blue-Nose Spell. It turned the medicine a bright blue at once. It really looked very pretty.

Chuckle pasted labels on each bottle: *MAGIC COUGH MEDICINE. ONE POUND EACH BOTTLE. WONDERFUL RESULTS.*

He put up a small table outside his front door, arranged the bottles on it, and then sat down to wait for customers. He winked at Ho, who was waiting at his door for people to come by. Then he was going to do his sweeping, and a cloud of dust would fly up and make the unlucky passer-by cough dreadfully.

Puckle the gnome came by, carrying a

shopping-basket. Ho took up his broom and swept the dust off his doorstep so that it went all over poor Puckle. Puckle looked round angrily. "What are you doing?" he roared. "Look at all this ..." But he couldn't go on because the Coughing Spell in the dust made him cough. How he coughed! Poor Puckle! He dropped his shopping-basket and all the eggs in it broke. He staggered about the road coughing wildly, and Chuckle called to him.

"Why, Puckle, what a dreadful cough you've got. You want some cough medicine. Try a bottle of mine."

Puckle staggered over to him, coughing. He put down a pound and took a bottle. He took out the cork, put the bottle to his mouth and drank. At once a peculiar expression came over his face, and his tongue hung out in disgust.

"Oooh! What horrible medicine. It's simply disgusting. Oooh!"

157

"Soon cure your cough though," said Chuckle. He knew that the Coughing Spell only lasted a minute or two. Puckle would think that the horrid medicine really had cured it. And, sure enough, he soon stopped coughing and went home.

"Take a dose every three hours," Chuckle called after him. "And I hope your nose turns blue tomorrow morning!" he added in a whisper.

Chuckle and Ho began to laugh as soon as Puckle was out of sight, but they soon stopped when they saw someone else coming along. It was High-Hat himself. Ha, ha! The two pixies were delighted to see their enemy. Now they would punish him properly.

Ho swept the dust violently from his doorstep again. High-Hat was just about to shout at him angrily when he swallowed some of the dust and the Coughing Spell got to work. He coughed instead, and his hat flew off his head.

"Dear, dear, High-Hat, you must have a cold coming on!" said Ho, and he ran to pick up High-Hat's hat. "You want some good cough medicine."

High-Hat soon saw the bright-blue medicine on Chuckle's table nearby and he rushed over to buy some.

This time Chuckle had a glass ready, and he poured High-Hat out a dose of his Magic Cough Medicine. High-Hat drank it off at once and paid a pound very willingly.

It wasn't long before the Coughing Spell wore off, and High-Hat really did think that it was the medicine that had cured it. "Wonderful!" he said. "Wonderful! Well, well, I'm glad to see that you are doing a bit of work at last, Chuckle. I hope I shall never have to tell you off again."

He went off, and the pixies laughed and laughed as soon as he was out of sight. "I'd love to see his blue nose tomorrow!" said Ho. "Sh! Here come two more people."

Well, that morning the two bad pixies swept Coughing Dust and sold Magic Cough Medicine to more than twenty people, so they made a great deal of money. When they shut up shop they

were full of glee. They counted out their money and planned what to buy with it.

"We've made a lot of money and we've punished the folk of Toadstool Town very well indeed," said Ho. "We'll play our trick again tomorrow."

But the next day was very very wet. The rain poured down, and it was no use at all putting a table of cough medicine outside Chuckle's front door. Also, the rain swept in at Ho's door as soon as he opened it, and turned the Coughing Dust into mud, so that it couldn't be swept into the air at all. "Well, we'll just have a nice lazy time at home today," said Ho, and he went to Chuckle's house.

Now, in Toadstool Town that

161

morning Puckle the gnome and High-Hat the pixie, and about twenty other people, had all wakened up with bright-blue noses. When they looked at themselves in their looking-glasses they almost fell over in horror. What had happened?

Of course, Puckle the gnome and all the others who had blue noses rushed round to tell High-Hat, because he was the head one of the village and would tell them what to do to make their noses pink again. When they saw that High-Hat has a blue nose, too, they were most astonished. They all began to talk about their blue noses. How had they got them? What had caused them?

It must have been a spell of some kind. But what spell? And then it all came out that each one of them had been covered with dust from Ho's broom, and had bought a bottle of Magic Cough Medicine from Chuckle.

"We all drank that medicine," said High-Hat, "and Chuckle must have put a spell into it. And there must have been a Coughing Spell in the dust that Ho swept over us. The bad, wicked fellows! As soon as we have got our noses right I shall go to them with the whole lot of you behind me, and we will all chase them round the village."

High-Hat made a spell in his biggest saucepan. When it smoked a bright pink colour he knew it was ready. He skimmed the scum off the top and then rubbed each blue nose with it. Immediately they turned back to pink again, and everyone was most relieved.

Then they set out for the pixies' toadstool houses. Some carried canes. Some carried spanking slippers. Some took sticks from the hedges. Look out,

Chuckle and Ho! You're going to have a bad time. In the pouring rain twenty very angry people went marching to see the pixies.

Ho happened to be looking out of the window, and he saw them. He gave a yell. "Chuckle! High-Hat and all the others are coming here with spanking slippers and canes! They've found out what we've done! Out of the back door, quick!"

They tore out of the back door just as

High-Hat rapped loudly at the front door. Into the pouring rain went the two pixies, not even waiting to put on coats or hats or take an umbrella. They had on bedroom slippers and these were soon soaked through. So were their thin tunics. But they didn't dare to go back home. No, High-Hat, and the others would be sure to be waiting for them!

By the time that night came both pixies had caught terrible colds. They sneezed and they coughed. Dear me – how they coughed! Almost as if they, too, had swallowed a Coughing Spell! They lost their way in the darkness, and presently they came to a tiny cottage. Coughing and sneezing, they went to the door to ask their way. An old dame with a very kind face opened it. When she heard them coughing she made them come in to the fire. "You're wet through!" she said. "Poor little things!"

Soon she had taken off their wet clothes and given them warm shawls to

wrap themselves in. She gave them hot soup and then popped them into her spare bed. "You stay here for the night!" she said. "I'll just go and get you a dose of cough medicine each. My nephew gave me a bottle today – he said it was wonderful!"

She brought them each a dose of medicine. The pixies felt too ill to notice that it was bright blue. They drank it up and lay back in bed thinking how horrible it had tasted. Thank goodness they had a shelter for the night, and need not go back home to face High-Hat and the others.

Now, it was Puckle who had given his old aunt the rest of the bottle of Magic Cough Medicine that he had bought the day before. That was before he had known what a dreadful trick it played, of course. The pixies had another dose later on, and then settled down for the night.

"Oooh! What horrible medicine it is!" said Chuckle, feeling sick each time he had a dose. "The very nastiest in the

world, I should think."

"It must be as bad as the Magic Cough Medicine you made!" said Ho, his tongue hanging out after he had drunk his dose. "And the worst of it is, it doesn't seem to make my cough better."

In the morning what a dreadful shock for Chuckle and Ho! Both of their noses were bright blue! The old dame gave a shriek when she came into the room and saw them.

"What's happened to you?" she cried. "I must get High-Hat at once! You've had a spell put on you!"

And before the frightened pixies could stop her she had sent somebody for High-Hat. He came along at once on his bicycle, cycling all the way from Toadstool Town. And when he saw the blue noses of Chuckle and Ho he laughed till the tears poured down his cheeks!

"So you had a dose of your own medicine, did you?" he cried, wiping his eyes. "What a joke! Oh, what noses you have!"

"Yours has gone pink again," said Chuckle, in a small voice. "Please, dear High-Hat, take the blue spell away from our noses, too. We'll never, never play such tricks again."

"Please don't punish us," begged Ho.

"Oh, I won't punish you myself," said High-Hat, beginning to laugh again. "Oh no – you've already been punished. You can keep your blue noses, both of you! And when people see the blue-nosed pixies they'll know who you are, and what a couple of bad fellows you've been, and they'll laugh fit to kill themselves. Ho, ho, ho! What a joke! The blue-nosed pixies!"

And off he went on his bicycle, roaring at the joke, longing to tell everyone else. As for Chuckle and Ho, they were dreadfully miserable. They coughed all day, and when at last they went home they took their blue noses with them in shame. And *how* everyone laughed at them. But it really did serve them right, didn't it?

The Kite
with a Tail

"Got you!" said a loud voice, and somebody pounced on Pippi the pixie.

"Oooh! Let me go!" yelled Pippi. "Help, help, where are you, Tricky? Help!"

"Tricky ran off when he saw me coming," said Sniff the goblin, holding Pippi tightly. "Oho! So I've got you at last, you mischievous little pixie. Always playing tricks on me and making me cross. Well, now I've caught you, and I shall take you home and keep you prisoner. I shall put a spell all round my house so that you can't possibly get away."

Pippi the pixie was dragged off by the goblin, who was twice as big as Pippi, and had a beard that almost reached the ground.

Tricky, Pippi's brother, watched from behind a tree. He was very scared. Sniff was a powerful goblin, and now he would make Pippi his servant, and never, never let him go. Oh, why had he and Pippi played tricks on him, booing at him from behind trees, and calling rude names after him?

"It's too late to think that now," said Tricky to himself. "What I've got to do is to try and find some way of rescuing Pippi."

But that wasn't at all easy. Sniff the goblin grew a high wall all round his little house and garden, so that nobody could possibly get in unless he let them in himself. There was a spell in the wall, and anyone who tried to climb it fell off with a bump long before he reached the top. Nothing could be thrown over the wall, because Sniff had put another spell at the top, and whenever anything was thrown up, it just came flying back.

Tricky ran everywhere to try and get

help for Pippi. But nobody could help him, because they knew how powerful Sniff's spells were, and they didn't know how to take the magic away from the wall.

Then one day Tricky met Cinders, his grandmother's black cat. She had green eyes and had belonged to a witch. She was an old cat now, and only wanted to laze by the fire, so the witch had sold her because she was no more use for helping to make spells.

"Hallo, Tricky," mewed Cinders. "How's Pippi?"

"Oh, didn't you know? He was caught by Sniff the goblin, and he's being kept a prisoner behind the high walls," said Tricky. "I simply don't know how to rescue him."

"Sniff the goblin? Now – let me see," said Cinders and her long whiskers twitched to and fro. "Yes, I remember now. He has a cat, as black as I am, with eyes as green as cucumbers. What's his name now – oh yes, Pad-About is my great grandson – or is it my great-great grandson? I forget."

Tricky waited patiently whilst the old black cat washed and went on talking.

"Now, you tell Pippi to say 'Creamy Buns' to Pad-About, and he'll know it's a message from me, and he'll help Pippi," said Cinders, beginning to lick her front thoroughly.

"'Creamy Buns!' What a funny message to send!" said Tricky.

"It isn't really. I once had Pad-About to stay with me, when I belonged to Witch Red-Cloak," said Cinders, "and he so far forgot himself as to eat a plate of creamy buns in the witch's larder. Well, they had a very strong spell in them and when I next saw Pad-About his furry head had turned into a cream bun. So I had to go and explain matters to the witch and beg for a spell to change him back."

"Good gracious! What a dreadful thing to happen to anyone," said Tricky, making up his mind never to eat

cream buns in a witch's house.

"Yes, it was. I felt so ashamed," said Cinders. "Such a thing had never happened in my family before. Pad-About was very, very grateful for my help. And whenever I want to send him a message and make sure that he knows it's from me, I say 'Creamy buns'. Pippi's only got to say that to him, and Pad-About will at once help him for my sake."

"Thank you very, very much," said Tricky, and went off happily. But he hadn't gone very far before he began to think how difficult it was going to be to get the message through to Pippi. How could he? He couldn't climb over the wall. He couldn't throw anything over because it just came back. He couldn't shout, or Sniff would know he was there and take him prisoner, too. Then how was he to get the message to Pippi?

"I'll send him a letter," thought Tricky at last. But no, that wouldn't do, because Sniff would be sure to read it.

176

Tricky went home, sighing as he tried to think of some good plan. Then someone called to him. It was little Hickory in the field beyond. "Hi, Tricky! Look at my lovely kite!"

Tricky looked. The kite flew up in the air and then, alas, dipped right down to the ground and lay still.

"It keeps doing that," shouted Hickory, sadly. "It just won't fly."

177

"You want a tail for it," said Tricky. "Come to my house and I'll make one for your kite."

So back they went to the house. Tricky cut up some paper, and showed Hickory how to fold it, and tie each piece to a long string, to make a tail.

"Wait," said Hickory, and he took a pencil out of his pocket. "I want to write a message on this tail – so that if my kite flies from me, and somebody else finds it, they will read my name and address on the tail."

So Hickory wrote on each piece of paper before he tied it to the tail. He put his name on the first bit – 'Hickory'.

He put half his address on the second bit – 'Hollyhock Cottage'. The other half went on the third bit – 'Cherry Town'. Then he put a word on each of the other bits that made the tail, so that his message read, 'Please return me my kite.'

"There! Aren't I clever?" he said, as he tied on the last piece.

Tricky stared at him, a wonderful idea coming into his mind. "Yes – you're *very* clever, Hickory. Cleverer than you think!"

179

And when Hickory had gone out happily to fly his kite with its new long tail, Tricky began to make a very fine plan of his own.

"I'll get a kite – and I'll make it a tail of bits of paper – tied to a string, like Hickory's – and I'll put one word on each bit of paper, so that if only I can fly it over the wall into Sniff's garden, Pippi will find it, and perhaps read the message!" Tricky was so thrilled with his plan that he danced all round the kitchen in joy.

He remembered that Pippi had a kite. That was fine! Pippi would know the kite, and guess there was some trick about its falling into Sniff's garden. Tricky thought he had better write a cheeky message on the kite's face, so that Sniff would see it and think Tricky had sent the kite just to be rude to him.

So he set to work. He got out the kite, which was a big one with a smiling face painted on it. He made it a fine new tail of bits of paper. There were twelve pieces, and Tricky wrote his message twice, one word on each piece of paper. This is the message he wrote:

"Say 'Creamy buns' to Pad-About. Say 'Creamy buns' to Pad-About."

Tricky grinned. What a silly message it seemed.

Never mind, it would work all right if only Pippi read it and acted on it.

He went out into the windy March afternoon. How the wind blew! Just the day for flying kites.

He went to the field that lay outside

Sniff's house. Up went the kite into the air. Besides the message on the bits of paper in the tail there was another message on the face of the kite itself. It really sounded very rude:

'Tell Sniff to put himself in the dustbin!'

Tricky grinned when he thought of that message. He felt sure that Sniff would be so angry when he saw it that he wouldn't even think of looking at the papers in the tail.

The kite flew high in the air, bearing its two messages. It flew right above Sniff's walled-in garden. Then Tricky jerked hard at the string, and the kite dipped down in surprise. Tricky let the string go loose – and the kite dipped in circles right down to Sniff's garden. It fell on the grass, and lay there, flapping a little in the wind.

Sniff was on it at once. "Ho! Somebody has sent a kite into my garden!" he stormed. "Go and get it, and bring it here, Pippi."

183

Pippi went to get it. He felt very frightened when he saw that it was his own kite, and that Tricky had scribbled such a rude message on it.

'Tell Sniff to put himself in the dustbin!" Oh dear, oh dear! What in the world would Sniff say?

Sniff said a lot. He shouted and yelled, and he boxed poor Pippi's ears till the pixie felt quite deaf. Then he flung the kite on the floor and jumped

184

on it till it was completely spoilt.

"If your brother thinks tricks of this sort are going to make me any kinder to you he can think again," roared Sniff. "Stupid, silly fellow!"

Pippi was very upset. He, too, thought it was very, very silly of Tricky. He sat in a corner, holding his ears, and moped.

Surely Tricky couldn't be so very stupid? Surely he must have sent the kite for something else besides a piece of mischief?

He sat and stared at the kite on the floor, its tail forlornly dragging behind it. And quite suddenly he saw part of a word written on one of the bits of paper that made the tail. His heart began to beat very quickly indeed.

"There must be another message on the tail – but a message for me this time," thought Pippi in excitement. "Tricky sent the rude message to attract Sniff's attention – but the other hidden message is for me. Oh, how can I manage to read it?"

He soon had his chance, because Sniff told him to take the kite and burn it on the kitchen fire. Pippi gathered it up and went into the kitchen, where Pad-About, Sniff's big black cat, was sitting dreaming by the fire.

"Move yourself," said Pippi, but Pad-About wouldn't. He was not a good-tempered cat, and had already scratched Pippi three times.

Pippi crammed the kite itself into the fire. He put all the tail into his pocket, and waited for Sniff to go out. As soon as the goblin had slammed the front door, Pippi took out the kite's tail, and with trembling fingers undid the bits of paper. He read the words on them.

'Say 'Creamy buns' to Pad-About. Say 'Creamy buns' to Pad-About'. Pippi stared at the extraordinary words. He could not make head or tail of them. He looked at them till he felt he could never forget them, and then he threw all the bits of paper into the fire.

He looked at Pad-About. Pad-About stared back, and then yawned widely.

"Creamy buns," said Pippi, suddenly. "CREAMY BUNS!"

Pad-About stopped yawning at once. He stared at Pippi as if he couldn't believe his ears.

"I said – 'CREAMY BUNS!" said Pippi. "Go on – it's a message for you. What about it?"

"It's a message from my great-great-grandmother, the black cat called Cinders, who used to belong to a powerful witch," said Pad-About, in a curious purring voice. "Only friends of hers know these words – 'Creamy

187

buns'. If you are a friend of hers, I must help you. I think you are a rude little pixie, but if my great-great-grandmother wishes it, I must be a friend to you."

"Good old 'Creamy buns'," said Pippi. "Well, Pad-About, I don't much like you either – you use your claws too much. But if you're going to help me, I'll change my mind about you. Now – how can you help me? Can you get me out of here?"

"Of course," said Pad-About. "See that bottle up there - full of yellow stuff. That's to make you small. Drink a teaspoonful, and you'll be small enough to go down that mousehole. It leads

under the house, down a tunnel and under the wall. It comes up the other side. You'll be free if you go down there."

"Thanks!" said Pippi, and drank a teaspoonful of the yellow stuff from the bottle. Immediately he felt as if he was going down in a lift, and everything became simply enormous round him. He had become as small as a mouse! He looked at Pad-About, who now seemed to be as large as an elephant, and looked exactly like a giant tiger!

189

Pippi decided to be very, very polite to him. "Thank you very much, Pad-About," he said. "If ever I can get a few creamy buns for you, I'll be delighted."

But that wasn't at all the right thing to say, and Pad-About at once put out a paw full of very sharp claws. Pippi shot down the mousehole in fright, and ran all the way till he came out under the wall, and found himself standing at the outlet of the hole in the field beyond. He had bumped into two or three startled mice, but that was all.

Still very small indeed, he tore across the field and after a long time he arrived at his own cottage. He hammered at the door, but couldn't make much noise with his tiny fist. Tricky heard him, though, and opened the door. He didn't see anyone at first, because Pippi was so very small.

"It's me – Pippi!" cried Pippi, in a voice as high and squeaky as a mouse's. Tricky couldn't believe his eyes. He picked Pippi up.

"You've gone small. Where's my Bigger Spell? Oh, here it is. Stay still Pippi, and let me blow it on you."

It wasn't long before Pippi was his own size again and the two gave one another a bear-like hug.

"You *were* clever to send that message on the kite's tail!" cried Pippi. "It did the trick! Pad-About just *had* to help me – and here I am!"

"What a shock for old Sniff!" said Tricky. "But all the same, Pippi, let's not play any more tricks on him. It's dangerous."

191

So they didn't – but I expect you know what they yell at poor old Pad-About whenever they see him? Yes – CREAMY BUNS!